MW00744437

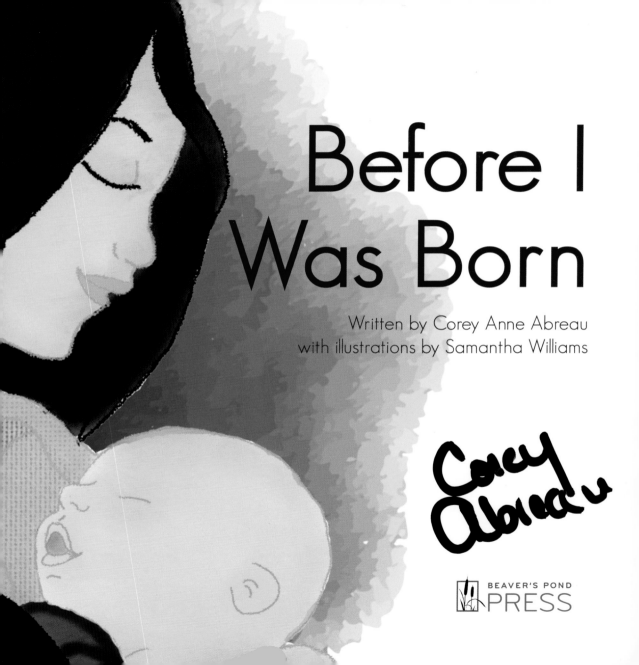

Before I Was Born

Written by Corey Anne Abreau
with illustrations by Samantha Williams

Beaver's Pond
PRESS

Edited by Lily Coyle
Illustrated by Samantha Williams

ISBN 13: 978-1-59298-598-2
Library of Congress Catalog Number: 2019906707
Printed in the United States of America
First Printing: 2019
23 22 21 20 19   5 4 3 2 1

Book design and typesetting by Dan Murphy

Beaver's Pond Press
7108 Ohms Lane
Edina, MN 55439–2129

(952) 829-8818
www.BeaversPondPress.com

To order, visit www.ItascaBooks.com
or call (800)-901-3480. Reseller discounts available.

Contact Corey Abreau at coreyabreau@gmail.com for speaking engagements, book club discussions, freelance writing projects, and interviews.

To my two boys, Carter and Cole. I love you both more than life itself.
-CAA

To my wonderful husband, Nabil. May we one day have a beautiful baby of our own.
-SW

side Mommy's belly I need nine months to grow.

Am I a boy or a girl?
Mommy can't wait to kno

verything alive starts out small as can be—
cluding vegetables, fruit, and babies like me!

MONTH 1

I'm barely the size of a papaya seed.
Mommy makes sure I get the nutrition I need.

MONTH 2

I'm the size of a grape, growing arms, legs, hands, and feet.
At the first doctor visit, Mommy hears my heartbeat.

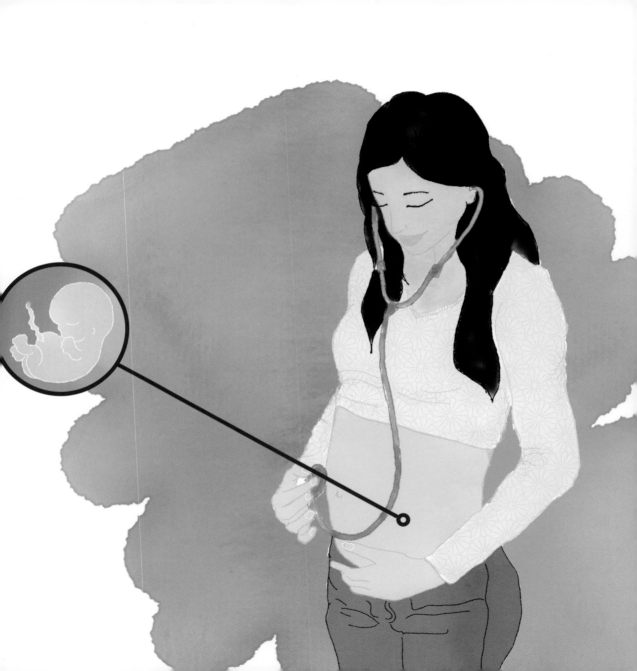

MONTH 3

I'm now the size of a plum!
I can scratch my nose and suck my thumb.

MONTH 4

I'm nearly the size of a pear.
I have eyebrows, eyelashes, and maybe some ha

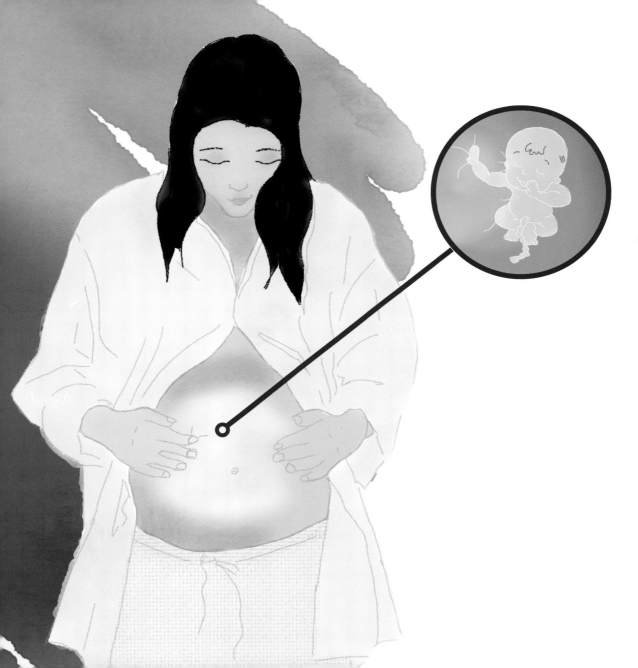

MONTH 5

m the size of a mango, weighing almost a pound.
stretch my body and wiggle around.

can also respond to a simple touch
you press Mommy's belly. (But don't press too much!)

Now the doctor can tell if I'm a girl or a boy—
ither way, Mommy is so full of joy!

MONTH 6

I'm just over one pound, like a ripe ear of corn.
I hiccup and kick and can't wait to be born.

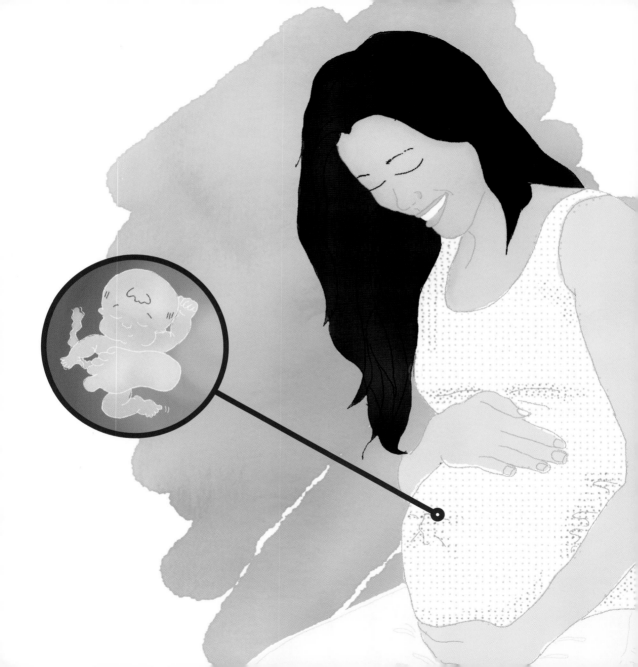

MONTH 7

I'm the size of an eggplant, close to two pounds.
My new family's voices are my favorite sounds!

Mommy tells me she loves me and we haven't even met.
This special growing time she will never forget.

MONTH 8

I'm about four pounds, the size of a squash.
All my energy makes Mommy say, "Oh my gosh!"

It's almost time to meet Mommy, and I hardly can wc
She'll know when I'm ready—I'll try not to be late!

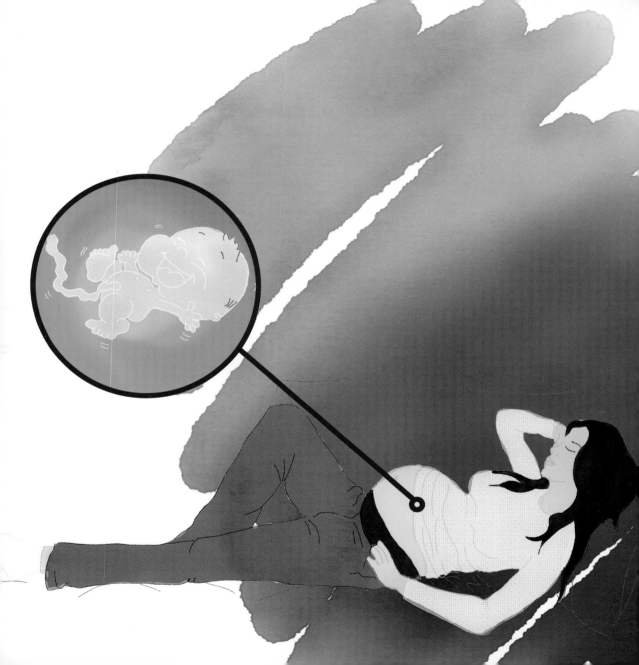

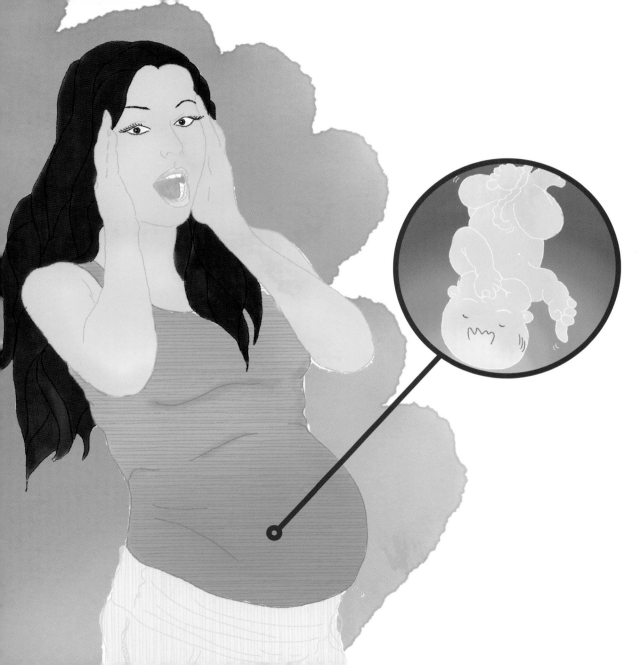

MONTH 9

I'm big as a watermelon, healthy and strong!
I can finally come out after growing so long.

I'm in Mommy's arms, where I've longed to be.
Am I done growing now? Just wait and see!